1

———————————

"To your promotion," Dom said, raising the glass of champagne. "New head of Gammatech's Safety Division."

Emily reached for her nearly-empty glass and held it aloft gently. "Thanks to you."

"I had hardly anything to do with it." Dom snatched the bottle from the bucket of ice and quickly topped off her champagne flute. "Management at Gammatech just knows a winner when they see one." He grinned and clinked his glass against hers. "You earned it."

Emily smiled and took a sip. She certainly had done everything in her power to prove herself at the energy company but that hadn't stopped the rumors and muttering behind her back—the whispers that she was only where she was because she had slept her way to the top. Dom laughed off the idea that anyone would doubt her resume, but no one had ever said anything to him directly. He was Dominic Del Toro, son of the owner of the company. He was immune.

Emily was not.

She had no doubt that there would be sideways glances on Monday when she was back at the office, but she was determined to enjoy the champagne anyway. She took another sip and took in the expansive view of the illuminated city skyline. She would enjoy tonight. Monday's problems could wait.

The server's reflection in the glass made her turn her gaze back to the bustling restaurant.

"Can I interest you in any dessert this evening?" He cleared away her plate and handed it off to a passing busboy.

"I actually hoped we could have the special tonight, Felipe. The one I called ahead about?" Dom said.

"Of course, sir." Felipe smiled. "I'll get that for you right away."

"Call-ahead special?" Emily asked. "Wow. Courtside seats at the game, now specialty desserts— you really did go all out tonight."

"Well, not quite yet," Dom said. He slid out of his seat and reached into his pocket as he stood. "There was one more thing I was hoping to discuss. One question that wasn't in your interview from the board yesterday."

Emily stared at the small black box in his hand. He was getting on one knee. Oh wow, this was happening now?

"Emily Marie Davis, from the first time I saw you, I was completely and utterly in love with you. Even all the way back at uni when you wouldn't give me the time of day." Dom smiled at her. "I would do absolutely anything to keep you in my life forever. Would you do me the honor of marrying me?"

Emily stared at the sparkling diamond as he opened the box, and realized her hand was shaking when some champagne sloshed onto the table. She hastily set the glass down.

"Oh my God. I can't believe you are doing this." Marriage. This was really happening.

He grinned up at her. "So, what do you say? Would you like to be Mrs. Del Toro?"

Emily looked into his eager eyes and slid out of her chair. Her breath seemed caught inside her, but finally she got the words out. "Yes, of course. Yes."

He stood to wrap his arms around her and she pressed her lips

CLOCKWISE & GONE

A TIME TRAVEL ADVENTURE

NATHAN VAN COOPS

Skylighter
Press

to his. Over the thrumming of her heartbeat in her ears, she registered the clapping and cheering of the other diners in the restaurant. But just barely. They may as well have been in another world.

The elevator ride to the street was a blur. She didn't even remember leaving the restaurant. There had been a dessert. A cake? She vaguely recalled that much. Another bottle of champagne had been opened too. That was still with them. Dom carried the half empty bottle with him to the car. As his vehicle pulled to the curb they climbed into the back laughing.

"Home, Avery," Dom managed, before Emily tackled him and started planting kisses all over his face.

"Proceeding to Regency Tower." The car's automated response system flashed the destination on a screen and engaged its drive motor.

Emily stopped kissing Dom long enough to admire the ring on her finger again. He'd really outdone himself this time.

"You like it?" Dom studied her with eager eyes.

"I love it. It's beautiful."

"Still doesn't compare to you," Dom replied.

As Emily reached for him again, the car's speaker came on and the voice of Dom's life management system, Avery, spoke. "A call coming in for you, sir. Inspector Walsh from subsection Delta."

"I'm a little busy right now," Dom replied between Emily's smothering kisses.

"He's all mine tonight, Avery," Emily said.

"The call is marked urgent," Avery replied. "How would you like me to respond?"

"Inspectors always think everything is urgent," Dom said. "Tell him I'll call him back."

"Yes, sir," Avery replied.

The car arrived at Regency Tower entirely too quickly as far as Emily was concerned. She had barely gotten Dom's tie off him, let alone anything else. He was altogether too buttoned up for her taste.

They were engaged. She had a fiance. It had seemed like a made-up word till now.

She let it roll around her mind as she carried her shoes and let Dom lead her toward the elevator. Her head was decidedly fuzzy from the champagne, but something about the ring on her finger was making him irresistible tonight. She entwined her fingers through his and leaned her head onto his shoulder in the elevator. He was wearing the cologne she'd gotten him for Christmas. She took a deep breath. Yes. This was going to be a good night.

Dom wasn't the most physically attractive man she had ever dated. If you had asked her yesterday she might even have said he wasn't in the top five. He lacked the height and athleticism she usually looked for. She had always dated ball players in college. Dom's physique was far better suited for a golf course than a basketball court. His jump shot was atrocious. He worked out when he could, but as heir to the Gammatech empire, he spent far more time in board meetings than at the gym. Add in the receding hairline, and Dom might even be considered homely by some. But what he lacked in looks he had more than made up for in devotion.

Ever since she moved back to the city, he'd been pursuing her. No. Longer than that. She could remember him trying to walk her home from parties in college, back before he'd lost his glasses. He'd always had style, and women interested in his money certainly fawned over him, but he used to show up to her games in a suit and tie. Not at all what she was looking for then. He'd even visited her in the hospital the night she tore her ACL and ended her dreams of going pro. Despite his continued attention, she'd barely given him a second glance. During the years since college she rarely thought of him at all unless it was at Christmas or her birthday. He always remembered to send a card. Real mail. Hardly anyone did that anymore.

Those were the little things that added up in the end.

When she finished with her energy contracts abroad and decided to search for a job back in the states, it was Dom that had contacted her immediately. He said he'd seen her resume and thought she'd be a wonderful fit at Gammatech. A management track with a salary that made competitor's offers look laughable. How could she say no?

The doors dinged open at the penthouse. His penthouse. Would they live here after they were married? The thought gave her pause. This was all happening so fast.

"Avery, please set lights to level 2," Dom said as they entered.

The normally bright lighting dimmed to a soft glow.

"Are you feeling okay?" Dom asked, smiling at her. Emily realized she was still latched to his arm and slowly unwrapped herself.

"Yes. But I think I need more champagne. You'll go find us some?"

Dom brushed a strand of her hair behind her ear. "I'm already as elated as I've ever been. More booze won't help."

Emily grabbed his hand and kissed his fingers. "Yes, but I need a minute to get sexy for you."

"You're already sexy," Dom grinned.

"Champagne," Emily commanded, pointing toward the kitchen. "Your fiancee says she needs champagne!"

He let go of her fingers and bowed, then turned toward the kitchen.

She did not need more champagne.

Her head was already swimming, but she was going to do this right. She pushed through the door to his bedroom and dropped her shoes near the closet doors. She should have planned ahead better. If she had known this was coming she would have tried to stash something here to wear. Something other than the yoga pants and old sweatshirt she kept stuffed in the bottom drawer of his dresser for nights she slept over. That wasn't going to cut it tonight.

She considered just stripping bare on the bed and waiting, but shook off the thought. She was feeling far too full from dinner to be up for that. She would opt for one of his button-down shirts. It wasn't lingerie, but he'd still like it. Can't beat the classics.

A cork popped from somewhere in the vicinity of the living room.

She ditched her dress on the floor and walked to the bathroom mirror to determine the appropriate amount of buttons to employ on the shirt. Once there she took a look at the state of her wavy chestnut hair and frowned. She was trying to get it back into some semblance of a style when Avery chimed from the other room.

"Call from Inspector Danvers, marked as urgent."

"Danvers?" Dom asked. "From Sector Echo?"

"Yes. There are also three other inspectors on the line. They've requested you join a community call. Shall I engage a video conference?"

"No!" Emily shouted from the bathroom. "He's busy."

"No video," Dom said as he walked into the bedroom.

"Hey, I'm not ready for you yet," Emily said. "You go there." She pointed him toward the bed.

"I might need to take this call," Dom said. "It sounds important."

"It's Saturday night. We just got engaged. Can't it wait?"

"I'm just going to see what's going on. Maybe it's nothing."

Avery chimed in. "Mr. Del Toro Senior has also joined the call but is requesting a private conversation."

Dom squeezed Emily's hand, then walked back into the other room.

Emily frowned and slumped onto the bed.

"Avery?"

"Yes, Miss Davis?"

"We're going to need to talk about his priorities . . ."

"I would be happy to provide any service Dom requires," Avery replied.

"I'll bet you would," Emily muttered.

She propelled herself off the bed and only wavered momentarily before pushing her way out the door to the living room.

Dom had his jacket back on and was attempting to retie his tie.

"You're leaving?" Emily said. "Where are you going?"

"I need to get down to the plant and check on things. This new shipment of cooling rods I ordered for the reactor is giving us some strange indications. The inspectors called a meeting. I guess it's pretty serious."

"Is everyone at the plant okay?"

"Yeah, absolutely. Just stay here. I'll be back as soon as I can." He finished the tie, then patted his jacket pockets, doing an inventory, before stepping over and kissing her. "Don't go anywhere."

"Fine," Emily said, pouting her lower lip, but adjusting his collar to better cover the tie.

He kissed her one more time, then slipped out the door. "Be back soon."

Emily stood staring at the closed door for a few seconds, then turned slowly on her heel to check her other options. The newly opened bottle of champagne was still sitting on the counter. She slouched over to it and snatched one of the glasses up before trudging back to the bedroom.

"Looks like it's just the two of us, Avery."

"Would you like to view entertainment options, Miss Davis? Perhaps the highlights from the afternoon's games?"

"Not tonight. I think I just want a bath. Will you fill the tub?"

"Bathtub will be filled in approximately eleven minutes. Would you like to choose a scent for your bath oils?"

"What does Dom use?"

"Mr. Del Toro prefers lavender and tea tree."

"Interesting. I'll try that." Emily took a sip of champagne. "And some music please." The penthouse filled with soothing instrumental piano music. "Something from this century," Emily said.

She was still bickering with Avery about the music choices when she heard the elevator ding in the hall. A moment later, footsteps sounded in the kitchen.

She opened the bedroom door and looked back out. "Dom?"

Dom had his back to her, rooting through a drawer in the kitchen, but turned around at the sound of her voice.

"That was fast," Emily said. "False alarm?"

He wasn't wearing a tie anymore. He looked . . . tired. Like the few minutes he'd been gone had aged him.

"Hello, Emily," Dom said. He stared at her, looking her up and down. "You look . . . well."

Well? She was half-naked in his shirt wearing a brand new engagement ring and 'well' was the best compliment he could muster?

"What happened?" she said aloud.

"We need to go," Dom replied. He strode across the room and grabbed her by the wrist.

"What? Go where?"

But he was already pulling her across the room toward the elevator.

"Dom, I can't go anywhere. I'm not dressed and it's late. I thought we were staying in. Ow. You're hurting me."

Dom's grip on her wrist was like a vice. He dragged her into the foyer. The elevator doors opened and he spun her inside.

"I don't have my shoes," Emily objected.

"You don't need them."

"Where are we going?"

He didn't reply. He was preoccupied with checking his phone. He studied the time, then shoved the phone back in his pocket. Emily stared at him but he seemed intent on ignoring her.

His face was stubbled. Hadn't he been clean shaven earlier tonight? Emily studied the shadow on his chin with confusion. How much champagne had she drunk? Things were getting strange.

The elevator reached the garage level and Dom hauled her forward across the oil-stained concrete to a waiting car. It wasn't his car, but Dom flung the door open without a moment's hesitation. "Come on. Get in."

"I want your jacket."

"What?"

8

"Give me your jacket. You're hauling me off to somewhere you won't explain. I'm not going in just your shirt."

"Why does it matter?" Dom asked. "We won't be seeing anyone."

Emily held out her hand for the jacket.

Dom sighed and took it off, then tossed it to her. He pushed her toward the car. Come on. We've got to go."

Emily climbed into the rear-facing bench seat and slipped her arms into the jacket. She wrapped it around herself and tucked her dirty feet up underneath her.

"Why on earth can't we just stay in the penthouse? What's the big hurry?"

Dom was glancing at his phone again. "You'll know soon enough. Avery, take us to Section Kilo."

"The research division?" Emily asked. Gammatech had what seemed like a thousand departments on a dozen campuses around the city, but she'd made a point of learning them all.

"Here. I need you to drink this." Dom held out a glass bottle of bright blue liquid. "It'll help you sober up."

"Then you drink it," Emily replied. "You're the one acting like a crazy person."

Dom shrugged, unscrewed the cap on the bottle, and took a swig. Then he held it out to her again.

Emily glared at him, but then took the bottle. Her head was beginning to throb. Hydration wasn't a bad idea. She took a sip and let the blue liquid course down her throat. It tasted like . . . What was it? Something she'd never felt. Like liquid lightning. Her throat tingled with it.

She considered Dom seated across from her. He was simply staring out the window. She sniffed and wrinkled her nose, then tried to locate the scent she was smelling. It was coming from his jacket. She lifted the collar and held it to her nose. Cologne. But one she'd never smelled before. When would he have had time to get more cologne? The bathtub hadn't even filled in the time he was gone.

She looked at her fiance across the back of the car. His expression was hard to read in the shadowy interior.

He *had* been clean shaven tonight. All those kisses.

"Dom?" she tried softly this time. "What's going on?"

When he looked at her, his eyes were serious. "You'll just have to trust me."

"But why can't you tell me what's happening? I'm getting frightened. You're freaking me out."

"Emily." He leaned forward and rested a hand on her knee. "In all the time you've known me, has there ever been anything I've done that wasn't in the interest of keeping you with me? Of keeping you safe?"

"No. Never."

"Then believe me when I tell you now. There is nothing I wouldn't do to keep you from harm."

"Are we in danger?" Emily asked.

Dom looked back out the window as the vehicle slowed. "Not for much longer. Drink the rest of that, then come on. We're here."

2

The concrete sidewalk leading to the research facility was cold on Emily's bare feet. She shivered a little and wrapped Dom's jacket around herself a little tighter. A security guard at the entrance tipped his hat to Dom.

"Good to see you again, sir. Twice in one night." He smiled and opened the door for them.

The doorway traded cold concrete for cold epoxy flooring that was slick beneath her feet.

Dom didn't slow his pace at all as he guided her through several hallways to what must have been the back of the building. He finally stopped at a doorway that had been chained shut and padlocked. Dom entered a combination and unlocked it, then pulled the entire chain free. Emily noticed that the combination had been her birthday, 4-9-20. Dom took a glance down the hallway they came from, then pulled the door open. "Okay. Here we go."

Emily wasn't sure what she expected, but the room they walked into wasn't it. It looked like an oversized storage closet. Dusty metal racks lined the walls, home for a few outdated computers and forgotten hard drives. There was a window on the far end of the room but the opaque glass squares only let in the faintest glow from the streetlight. Dom flipped the switch and illuminated the room with harsh fluorescent light.

He ran the chain through the door handles again and refastened the lock.

"About time," someone said. "I thought you said you'd be quick."

Emily located the speaker sitting in a folding chair in the corner. He rocked forward and stood, shaking out the length of his overcoat and stomping his feet. He was skinny, dressed in all black, and smoking an electronic cigarette. She hadn't seen one of those in years.

"Why are you just lurking here in the dark?" Dom said. "It's creepy."

"You wanted me to stay here. I stayed. You didn't say you needed me awake."

Dom turned toward Emily. "This is a new acquaintance of mine. What did you say your name was again?"

"Axle."

"Well, Axle, did you at least prepare things for me like I asked you to?"

"Setup's all ready. Standard stuff." He pointed to a rolling office chair and a contraption against the wall that looked like some kind of door frame.

"Dom, what's going on?" Emily said. "You really need to tell me what we're doing here. Who is this guy?"

"We're getting away for a little," Dom said. "I've got somewhere where we can go to get things sorted out. I've got a way to keep you safe."

Emily noticed that Axle was eyeing her bare legs and tried to tug the edge of Dom's jacket a little lower.

"You don't mind me saying so, mack, you got a fine looking lady here. Lots going for you. You sure you don't want to just forget this plan and go off and enjoy her somewhere? I'm thinking I would."

"Shut your damn mouth," Dom growled at him. "I didn't pay you for your suggestions. I paid you to do your job. Just get things ready. We're wasting time."

Axle held up his hands. "Whatever you say, mack. You're the boss." He stepped over to the doorframe erected by the wall and started fiddling with a control panel attached to the side. A number of heavy-duty cables were running across the floor and were directly wired into the breaker box on the wall.

"Emily, I need to tell you something," Dom said. "I'm sorry to keep you in the dark about this but we're almost safe. There is going to be a problem at the plant. The reactor core is growing unstable. It's going to . . . It's going to do a lot of damage. But I have somewhere to take us. I can fix things. I just need you to come with me. It's all going to be okay."

"The main reactor?"

As she spoke, the door frame against the wall started buzzing. The space between the posts began to shimmer, then erupted into a field of multicolored light. The colors swirled and twisted in an eerie sort of harmony with one another. Emily found herself transfixed by their beauty.

"What is that?" she murmured.

"Our future," Dom replied. "Have a seat."

Dom wheeled a rolling office chair over and Emily sat, almost automatically, her eyes still glued to the luminescent doorway. She didn't look away until something cold closed over her wrist. She looked down to find her arm handcuffed to the chair.

"Hey, what the hell?"

"Standard procedure," Axle muttered from next to her..

"Procedure for what?" Emily demanded.

Dom shoved Axle out of the way and knelt in front of Emily. He rested a hand on her knee, then held up another bottle of blue liquid. "I need you to drink this."

"What the hell is that stuff, Dom? And don't give me that 'sober you up' bullshit."

"It's going to help stabilize your cells," Dom replied. "The more we get into you, the safer you'll be."

Axle wheeled an IV rack over to her chair and started prepping a syringe.

"You have got to be kidding," Emily replied. She snatched the bottle from his hand and threw it across the room. "I'm not drinking anything until you explain what you're doing to me."

Dom closed his eyes for a moment, then grabbed her arm and took her hand between his. "Emily." He opened his eyes again and stared into hers. "That machine over there is going to take us somewhere new. But in order to get there, we need to treat your body with a special sort of particle. It will protect you and enable you to travel safely. But only if we get enough into you to make it work."

"Why aren't you cuffed to a chair? Why isn't he?" She looked to Axle who was now wheeling some other contraption made of hollow tubing toward them.

"We've already had our treatment," Dom replied. He kissed her hand then laid her forearm against the arm of the chair. "Now I need you to stay still." He wrapped a fabric strap quickly around her arm and fastened the Velcro.

"Hey! No. Dom!" Emily tried to jerk her arm loose but it was strapped tight. She tried moving her other arm but the metal handcuffs only rattled against the chair. "I don't want to do this. Let me go!"

"There is no other way," Dom replied. He grasped her face between his hands. "Your future depends on this."

"Dom." She stared at him with her most no-nonsense expression. "I want to go home. Let. Me. Go."

But Dom simply strapped a band around her other arm and secured it tightly to the chair as well. Axle bent down with the needle.

"Get that away from me!" she shouted.

"It's going to hurt more if you move," Axle replied. He pressed on the inside of her arm, probing for her vein.

"Don't you touch me with that—" she began, but it was too late. He already started inserting the needle. She froze. When the IV was in, he taped the tube to her arm and stood up.

She caught him staring down her shirt. She jerked against the arm of the chair but it was no use. Why hadn't she used . . . more . . . buttons . . .

She felt dizzy. Her head lolled slightly.

"What else did you put in there?" Dom asked.

"Just something to calm her down. Figured we may as well get a head start on the rest of it."

Dom frowned but didn't object. He stood, and swayed with the rest of the room as it turned. It was all getting wavy.

Emily's pulse was throbbing in her ears with the rhythm of a clock but the men seemed to be moving in slow motion. She tilted her head as Axle wheeled the tubular structure overtop of her seat. It was a sort of framework, bolted together with space in the interior for her, and with what looked to be plastic sheeting around the edges. She felt like she was in a portable shower. A bright light illuminated the sheeting. It was clear, but difficult to see through. The room had been going blurry before, but now it was even more difficult to see. Dom was just a vague shape on the other side of the curtain.

"Dom?" Her voice came out softer than she intended. She meant to yell at him but it only sounded like pleading.

"Where are you—" the air crackled with static and blue light flickered around the curtain. She saw now that it wasn't plastic, but rather some sort of conductive material ribbed with fine strands of metal. Electricity danced and tingled across her skin and seemed to burn through her veins. She cried out from the shock of it.

Moments later it was over.

The two men were muttering something on the other side of the curtain, continuing to ignore her, when a loud bang erupted near the doorway. A blinding light flashed, causing her to squint and blink, and then there were voices. The overhead lights went out.

Her ears were ringing. Axle shouted. Something crashed to the floor amid a scuffle ahead of her.

"Get her loose!" a man shouted.

Someone collided with the curtain and she caught a glimpse of Axle, snarling and drawing a knife from his belt. The multicolored light emanating from the strange doorway behind her was barely enough to see anything, but she felt hands on her right arm, someone unwrapping the Velcro straps.

"Dom?"

But it wasn't Dom. A face in a black ski mask appeared in front of her. They unstrapped her other arm.

"Listen, you have to run!" It was a woman's voice.

"No! Don't touch her!" Dom shouted as he flung the tubular framework aside and grabbed for the woman in the mask. She backed away and he pursued her, fist raised.

Emily tried to rise from the chair but her left arm was still hand-cuffed to it. She wobbled and sat back down. What had they given her?

She was about to try again, but then Axle was there, his leering expression illuminated by the eerie flickering light. "You ain't going anywhere, honey. Except gone." He put a hand on the chair arm, and the other over her handcuffed wrist. Then he pushed her, hard, toward the multi-colored doorway. His hand ripped the IV from her arm as he shoved. "Have a nice trip!"

"No, wait!" Dom shouted.

Emily attempted to plant her feet to stop her momentum but her bare heels just slid across the slick epoxy floor. The wheels of the office chair wobbled but her trajectory was true. She rolled right into the swirl of light and color.

There was a fraction of a moment where she felt like she'd departed her body and was soaring through the cosmos.

Then the wheel of the office chair hit something and she tipped, nearly spilling out of it onto the floor. The chair teetered, then settled back onto its wheels, planting her in the seat in a room once again filled with fluorescent light. There was a medical table, some silver trays on wheels, and someone standing in front of her. She looked up to find a man in paper scrubs and latex gloves looming over her. He was wearing a paper mask and had a foot jammed against one of the chair's wheels.

"Well, what did Axle bring us today?" the man asked.

Footsteps sounded from behind her and when she spun around in the chair she found a second masked doctor on her other side. He was holding a scalpel. "Not bad looking, this time," he said. "Pity. Get her on the table. Let's open her up."

3

There was a some kind of drug in her system. It was making her dizzy. Added to the bottles of champagne from dinner and the chaos she'd been through since then, Emily was not feeling her best. But despite those limitations, there was no way in hell she was going down without a fight.

As the masked doctor dragged her to her feet by her arm, she looked for options. She had next to none. She waited till the other doctor leaned over to unlock her handcuffs, then she kneed him in the face.

Leaned over the chair, the man's nose crunched as the top of her knee connected with it. The man holding her up scrambled to get a better grip on her but he was too slow. She used her planted foot and rammed backwards, knocking into his face with the back of her head. It had the desired effect. He let go of her to protect his face.

That was as far as she'd gotten with her plan, but it bought her a second or two and enough room to move. Her timing with the kick had been off. She was still handcuffed to the chair. She grabbed the arms of the chair and lifted it, smashing it into the man she had kneed in the face. He staggered back, still holding his nose.

An exit sign hung over a door on the far wall. She ran toward it, knocking over trays of instruments and a cooler full of ice packs in the process.

"Get her!" the man with the bleeding nose sputtered.

The other doctor had reached the wall and grabbed something from a shelf that looked like some sort of Taser. The crackle of electricity a moment later confirmed it. Emily wrestled with the doorknob while attempting to carry the office chair one-handed. She finally got the metal door to swing inward and was confronted with her next obstacle. Stairs.

This medical facility appeared to be located in the basement, with concrete steps leading up to a street. She took a firm grip on the chair and bounded up the stairs into soft morning light. She wavered a bit at the top, dropping the chair back onto its wheels. The rush of blood was making the world spin. The sky was light blue with white puffy clouds drifting in the breeze, but the sun was just coming up over a distant hilly horizon. Narrow three story row houses densely packed the sloped street and ran downward toward a traffic light. What part of the city was this? And how was it morning already?

The pounding of footsteps behind her made her move.

She sprinted down the barren sidewalk half dragging the chair behind her. The doctor emerged onto the sidewalk and glanced around. Emily looked for help but the street was deserted with the exception of cars crossing the intersection down the hill.

"Hey! Somebody!" She screamed but the cars were too far away and immune to her pleas.

The doctor headed toward her. He pulled the mask from his face to reveal a stubbled square jaw and cleft chin. He was glaring as he began jogging, and then running after her, the Taser poised in one hand.

Emily pumped her free arm, her bare feet slapping the concrete as she ran, but it was difficult. The chair she was dragging kept rolling into her heels to trip her up and the steady decline was making it hard to gain speed without toppling over.

Plus whatever they had drugged her with was making her sluggish.

The doctor was almost on top of her. He stretched out a hand for her shoulder. "Get back here!"

Emily put on a burst of speed, and in a desperate maneuver, swung the office chair around in front of her and leapt onto it, attempting to steer it with her weight on her knees.

It was working!

She barreled away from her pursuer, picking up speed as she flew down the sidewalk. A man was standing on a doorstep ahead of her. Where had he come from? With bright red hair and a jacket for a sports team she vaguely recognized, he walked off the doorstep and into her path.

"Watch out!" she screamed.

She cringed as she flew toward him, closing her eyes at the moment of impact, but a moment later, she realized it hadn't happened.

She opened her eyes to find her path clear. The man had somehow avoided the collision and was now behind her, blocking the path of the man chasing her. The doctor had trouble slowing his speed and the red-haired man sent a fist into his face at full force.

"Yes!" Emily shouted. But her elation immediately vanished when the wheel of her office chair hit an uneven edge of sidewalk. The chair overturned and sent her sprawling to the concrete. The chair followed her as she tumbled, rolling overtop of her before slamming into the sidewalk on the other side. The arm of the chair broke free and the rest of the chair skidded a few more feet down the hill. Emily rolled over and got gingerly to her feet. Her elbow was burning, her knee and the top of her right foot as well, but the scrapes looked mostly superficial. She cringed as she stood, brushing bits of concrete from the wounds. When she looked up, she was shocked to find that both of the men behind her were gone.

She stared at the vacant space where she had seen the red-haired man punch the doctor, but it was empty. No. Not quite empty. The paper mask the doctor had been wearing was lodged in a tuft of weeds growing near the gutter. But the men were nowhere to be seen.

A car came down the hill, cruising by slowly, but the passenger was absorbed in some device or another in their lap and paying no attention to the outside world.

Emily hobbled up the hill a little, glancing at the closest doorways to see if the men had entered one of the houses, but then quickly turned and continued downhill, eager to get away from the scene.

She was a mess. She'd ripped a hole through Dom's jacket and shirtsleeve at the elbow, a rivulet of blood was coursing down her bare leg from her knee, and her foot was bleeding as well. She was leaving a bloody footprint as she walked.

That wouldn't do. She wasn't going to leave a trail for the other doctor to find her. She might have broken his nose, but his eyes still worked.

She limped as far as the next intersection, turned the corner of the block, then looked around for the nearest smart surface. A Digi-Com logo on a window caught her eye and she staggered over. She raised her left hand to touch the window but the chair arm still handcuffed to her wrist made it too awkward. She switched to her right hand instead, tapping the windowpane with a fingertip. A generic menu of common apps appeared on the window-turned-screen and she tapped the logo for a local public car service. She pressed her thumb to the screen when prompted and her private passenger profile popped up. The windowpane didn't appear to be wired for audio so she was required to manually select a destination. Her frequented sites appeared. Dom's apartment. Her office at Gammatech. Home. But when she tapped the home button, the address displayed on the screen was incorrect. It listed a building in Highland Park downtown, somewhere she had never lived.

"What the hell?" Emily frowned at the screen and simply swiped the destination away, manually entering her address instead. She hastily pressed the call button and got an immediate ping back from a public car in her area. At least she was beating the commuter traffic.

Emily quickly logged out of the smart screen and limped to the curb.

There was still no sign of the doctor who had pursued her, or her red-headed savior.

The car pulled up to the curb only moments later and the door opened automatically. Casting one last look around, she gingerly climbed inside and shut the door.

The car started rolling.

Thank God.

The realization of what she had just survived was pressing in on her and she had to keep herself from shaking. She put her hands to her head but the arm of the office chair thunked against her thigh, reminding her that she was still dragging a piece of the experience along with her. She grabbed at the triangular-shaped chair arm and tried to find a way to get it free from the handcuffs. The frame of the arm was continuous however, and short of a hacksaw, it wasn't going to come free.

She leaned back in the seat and stared at the ceiling. One problem at a time.

The scene she had just lived replayed in her mind.

What on earth was Dom thinking? Did he know these doctors were on the other side of the doorway? What was that door even made of? Wherever she was, it was miles away from the Gammatech facility they had started in. Had Gammatech been developing some kind of teleportation technology? Why had she never heard about it?

The questions were overwhelming.

She tapped the car window to open another smart screen. She opened a call line but hesitated over Dom's profile picture. Should she call him to see what was going on? What if he was organizing this whole thing and tracked her call? No matter how hard she tried, she couldn't understand how this situation made any sense. This was Dom she was talking about, her fiance—the most devoted man she had ever been with. Never in all the time she had known him had he ever done anything to harm her. It was the opposite. He did everything for her, cherished her, almost to the point of obsession . . .

She closed the phone app.

The car pulled onto her street and began to slow, but something looked wrong. Emily couldn't exactly put her finger on it but the neighborhood looked . . . different. Nothing specific stuck out to her, but there was definitely something off.

When the car pulled to the curb in front of her apartment building, she got out cautiously. It was still early but there were lights on in the building. Some of her neighbors were definitely awake. She didn't relish the idea of trying to explain her appearance to any of them. Luckily everyone still had their blinds down.

She made a futile attempt to wipe her bloody handprint from the seat using the sleeve of Dom's jacket, but gave up and limped her way to the front steps. The car company could bill her if anyone complained. She just needed to get inside.

When she reached the door and stuck her thumb to the access pad, the lock beeped at her and flashed red. Frustrated, she wiped her thumb on the jacket and tried again. The red light flashed again.

"Let me in, you stupid piece of—"

"It won't work."

Emily jolted and spun around. The red-haired man was standing casually on the sidewalk behind her as if his miraculous appearance there was the most commonplace thing in the world. He took a step forward.

"Get away from me!" Emily brandished the chair arm at him. "Don't you touch me!"

The man held up his hands and took a step back. "Hey. Just trying to help. I'm on your side."

"Who the hell are you?" Emily snapped. "And how did you follow me?"

The man slowly lowered his hands and rested them at his sides. "I'm sorry to tell you, but this isn't your house."

"What?" Emily tried to process what he was saying.

"You don't live here," he replied. "Not anymore."

"Bullshit," Emily said, pressing on the keypad again with her thumb. She pressed harder this time. The aggravating red light flashed again. She continued to hold the chair arm toward him.

"Do you want me to get that off for you?"

Emily eyed him suspiciously. "You have the key?"

"No. But I have something just as good." He reached into the pocket of his jacket and extracted a metallic cylinder about the size of a small flashlight.

"What is it?"

"It's called a degravitizer."

"That sounds like a word you just made up."

The man slowly took a step closer. "I don't have to touch you. But if you just want to step a little closer, I can use it on the cuffs."

Emily continued to eye him cautiously but his bright blue eyes seemed sincere. She vacillated for another moment, then held her breath and took a step closer.

He gently grasped the chair arm between two fingers to hold it steady, then aimed one end of the flashlight-looking device at the chain holding the two cuffs together. He pressed a button on the device.

Nothing seemed to be happening but the man moved the device confidently, working his way along the chain to the section of metal just below her wrist. He was careful not to aim it at her hand. She didn't see why, because when he pulled his hand away, the handcuffs seemed as intact as ever.

Emily shook her wrist. "How ever will I repay you for your incredible locksmithing services?"

The man smirked at her. "I'm not done yet." He slipped the

device back into his pocket, then pushed up the sleeve of his jacket to reveal a wristwatch. At least it resembled a wristwatch. It looked more complex than any timepiece Emily had seen before, with several extra dials and indicators. He moved one of the dials just slightly. "Okay, this is the part that you do need to touch me for. You can grab my shoulder if you like."

Emily considered his request, but not seeing how it would change their situation for the worse, laid her free hand on his shoulder.

"You might want to close your eyes. Some people get dizzy at this part."

"I'm already dizzy," Emily replied. "I'll be keeping them open."

"Have it your way." The man reached for his wrist and pressed a button on the side of his watch.

Emily blinked. Or at least it felt like she did. She was fairly certain that her eyes had stayed open the entire time, but it was almost as if the world had blinked.

The man was smiling.

Emily failed to see what he was grinning about, as her wrist was still handcuffed. But then she noticed it. The section of the cuffs he had waved his magic wand thingy over was missing. More accurately, it was now lying in several pieces on the sidewalk near her feet. She moved her wrist, backed up a step, and the handcuff slipped open, the guts of its locking mechanism now relocated to the ground.

Emily's mouth dropped open. After a moment of trying to comprehend what had just happened, she looked up into the man's smiling blue eyes.

"Who are you?" she finally managed.

He took the remnant of the chair from her and held out his hand. "My name's Carson. I'm a time traveler, and I'm here to help."

4

"There's no such thing as time travel," Emily said.

Carson smiled at her. "I beg to differ."

Emily appraised him skeptically. "Thanks for unlocking me. I think you should go now."

"You need help," Carson replied.

Emily couldn't really argue with that statement. Standing on the steps of her apartment building bleeding all over the stoop was all she had going for her at the moment. She couldn't even get inside.

"Are you a crazy person?" she asked.

"I'm not," Carson replied.

"Are you lying to me?"

"No. I'm not."

"Prove it."

Carson smiled. "Prove what? That I'm not crazy or that I'm not a liar?"

"You said you were a time traveler. You're either crazy, you're lying, or you're actually telling the truth. So prove it. Time travel."

Carson put his hands in his pockets. "I just did. You're out of those cuffs, aren't you?"

"Magically disintegrating things is not time travel," Emily said.

"They could have been trick handcuffs or something. You could be a circus magician. That's not the same thing."

Carson nodded. "Okay. What size are you?"

"What?"

"In clothes." He looked down at her bare legs.

"That's none of your business." She wrapped Dom's jacket a little tighter and clenched the neck closed with one hand.

"Fine. But you can't blame me if they don't fit. Hold this." He handed her the piece of chair again, then he walked over to the railing at the side of the steps and rested a hand on it. "Don't go anywhere. I'll be right back." With one hand on the railing, and the other on his wristwatch, he promptly disappeared.

Emily took a step back.

"What . . . the . . ."

But then he was there again. She barely had time to register it, but there he was, still touching the railing. Now he was holding a shopping bag. A shopping bag pulled from thin air.

"Holy shit," she muttered.

"I brought you some options," he said, rummaging around in the bag. "And a first-aid kit." He held up a white plastic box with a red cross on it. "You want to get cleaned up?"

Emily stared at the bag then looked up at his face. He was acting like it was no big deal. That red hair, his laughing blue eyes. A time traveler. He just vanished and came back with clothes? This man was entirely too impossible to be believed.

She didn't know if it was her adrenaline ebbing, the drugs taking hold or just plain exhaustion, but her knees began to shake. She wobbled once, then again, trying to regain her balance.

"Whoa there." The man dropped the bag and reached for her as she began to faint. The world seemed to narrow around him, until it left just his face, and then his mouth. "I did say it might make you dizzy."

She felt his arms slip around her waist, then she surrendered to the black.

When she woke up, Emily was lying on a bed. She was fairly certain she had never been in this room before, but there was something very familiar about it. She liked the curtains at least.

She stayed horizontal while getting her bearings, but she felt better. The effects of whatever had been in her system seemed to have worn off. Her head felt clear again. Or at least as clear as it could be considering the circumstances. She wanted to believe that the entire experience had been just a bad dream, but that wasn't an option. She was here. This room that was strange and yet familiar.

At least she was clothed.

Someone had cleaned her up. She propped herself up to an elbow, winced, then remembered her injury. She pushed up the sleeve of the white cable knit sweater she was wearing and found that her elbow had been neatly bandaged. Her leg had been bandaged too. She could feel the lump at her knee beneath the jeans someone had put on her, and her right foot was carefully wrapped in a bandage that went all the way up her ankle. She could flex it, but it was securely affixed.

A full glass of water was perched on a coaster on the nightstand. She picked it up and took a precautionary sniff, then sipped at it.

Oh that was good.

She hadn't noticed how dehydrated she was at first, but the more she drank the more she realized she needed it. She set the glass down and tried sitting up. She slowly let her legs dangle over the edge of the bed till her feet touched the floor. It was cool and soothing.

The room was well lit and sunny. It had to be at least midday. Had she been unconscious that long? Perhaps just asleep. She tried to remember what day it was. Saturday? No, Sunday now. Had to be. She slid forward and pushed herself to her feet.

The bedroom door was open a crack. Somewhere on the other side, there were voices speaking quietly. She crept gingerly across the rug, then paused briefly when she passed in front of the mirror. The cozy sweater kept sliding off one shoulder, but otherwise she looked good. Clean. Rested. Her finger sparkled in the sunlight and she held up the engagement ring.

Where was Dom right now? Was he searching for her?

She let her hand drop and moved toward the door. She peered through the crack in the doorway, searching for the source of the voices. Not seeing anyone, she cautiously opened the door.

The living room was decorated with a wide couch, seasonal fall decorations and tasteful artwork. She recognized a worn blanket on the couch as one that she herself owned. Whoever lived here must shop at the same stores. She moved into the kitchen and admired the view out the broad windows.

She was many floors up. A condo of some kind with a patio overlooking downtown.

The voices she had heard were coming from a second bedroom but she couldn't make out much of what was being said.

There was a butcher's block on the countertop with a set of knives. She eased over to it and gently removed one of the smaller blades, then hid it in the sleeve of her sweater. If there were more surprises here, she meant to be ready.

She moved out of the kitchen, looking for the exit, but as she did so, the door to the patio slid open automatically for her, making enough noise to alert whoever was in the other room that she was awake. The voices stopped.

She still hadn't located the front door so she stepped onto the patio instead and backed away from the doorway, giving herself a little room to maneuver. She kept the knife gripped tightly in her fingers underneath the loose-fitting sweater.

A jacket was laid over one of the patio chairs. The logo for the team mascot was green and gold. Carson's jacket.

When no one immediately appeared, she walked the edge of the walled patio. Far below her, tourists and office workers were going about their day. It was just another day in the city. She scanned left and looked north of downtown, her eyes searching for the usual landmark of her day, the Gammatech building. But when she located the building, she was surprised to see a different name on the top, Sunspire Lending. Emily frowned and studied the sign. Had someone else purchased the building overnight?

That sign being up already was fast work by anyone's standards.

"How are you feeling?"

Emily spun around to find Carson standing by the open sliding door holding a pair of coffee mugs.

She tucked the hand with the knife behind her back. "Better. Thank you. Do I owe you for that?"

"The least I could do. You had a rough night."

Emily nodded. Since it seemed, at least for the moment, that he wasn't planning to assault her, she turned her attention back to the view. "Do you know anything about the Gammatech building? Did someone buy the sponsorship last night?"

Carson looked north to the building she was referencing. "Yeah. Something like that. You want any coffee? I poured you a cup but I didn't know if you wanted anything in it."

"Black is fine. Thanks." Emily walked toward him and they met at the patio table. She took one of the mugs with her left hand and raised it toward him. Carson clinked his against it and smiled. He took a sip.

"Where are you from?" Emily asked, eyeing the jacket draped over the chair. "Is that University of South Florida?"

"Go Bulls." Carson replied.

"Is this your place?"

"No. Just visiting," Carson said. "Doing a favor for someone. Well, a job really."

Emily's eyes drifted toward the interior of the condo where she had heard a woman's voice. "Are you married?"

"No. It's just me at the moment," Carson replied. His eyes lingered briefly on her engagement ring. "But I do have a friend inside that I'd like you to meet. She's the reason I brought you here."

Emily stood up a little straighter. "Oh really. Why is that?"

Carson sipped his coffee again. "You'll see. I should probably let her explain it." He walked back through the patio door into the kitchen. Emily followed.

When Carson reached the door to the other bedroom, he paused and turned around. "It's okay if this feels strange. It's perfectly normal to feel that way at first."

Emily eyed the door cautiously. "Are they naked in there or something?"

Carson smiled. "No. Nothing like that, it's just . . . Well, I guess you'll just have to see."

He opened the door for her. Emily tried to read his expression but couldn't figure out what he was getting at. She kept the knife in her hand ready beneath her sleeve, but as she entered the room, a number of strange things caught her eye. For one, there was a framed photo of her parents sitting on the desk near the door. The dresser was one she had at home in her apartment, and there was a picture of the dog she had in college sitting atop it.

What the hell?

The bedspread was hers as well. But these things didn't prepare her for the woman lying in the bed. Her hair was thin and her skin was pale, but the face looking back at her was immediately recognizable. She'd seen it looking back at her from mirrors her entire life.

Emily dropped her coffee mug and it bounced off the knotted rug before spilling its contents all over the floor.

"Hello, Emily. It's good to see you." The woman spoke softly, ignoring the mug. She was propped up in bed by a number of pillows and sunlight was streaming through the blinds to illuminate her face. She smiled.

"You're . . . you're . . ." Emily stammered.

"That's right. I'm you," the woman replied. "And we have a lot to talk about."

31

5

"**Y**ou might want to take a seat for this," the Emily in the bed said. She gestured toward the armchair near the foot of the bed. Emily looked at the puddle of coffee she had created on the floor but the woman waved her hand. "Don't worry about that. We can take care of it later."

Emily was still speechless. She sat down slowly, feeling vaguely awkward about how much she was staring, but she couldn't help it. She couldn't take her eyes off this woman in the bed. Her face. It was surreal and amazing and terrifying all at the same time. The woman's reassuring smile helped. She waited patiently till Emily sat before speaking again.

"I know you've had a very difficult day. Lots to take in. For what it's worth, I think you're handling it admirably well."

"I don't think I even know where to start with this," Emily replied. "With . . . you. It's like I'm living in Wonderland or something."

"It *is* a bit of a temporal rabbit hole," the other Emily said. "Do you know where you are?"

"Downtown. Highland Park?"

"No. I meant, do you know when you are?"

Emily shook her head. "I don't know what you mean. Isn't it . . .Sunday?" The question sounded feeble coming out of her mouth. What had happened to her life that she was now so unsure of basic facts, like what day of the week it was? She felt completely ungrounded here.

"It's 2048," the woman said. "It's been five years since the night you got engaged."

"Five years?" Emily looked out the window at the distant skyline. She could see the Gammatech building. It wasn't overnight. It was like Carson had said. Time Travel.

The Emily in the bed shifted her weight to sit up a little straighter and grimaced a little as she did so.

"Are you okay?" Emily asked. "Do you need help?"

Her other self gave a wan smile and refolded her hands in her lap. "I need a lot of help. That's actually why I asked Carson to bring you here." She looked around the room and then finally her eyes came back to Emily. "There's so much to say that I almost don't know where to start, but I suppose it's best to just tell you from the beginning. This has a lot to do with Dom."

"I thought it might," Emily said. "He just went crazy tonight. Or . . . whenever."

"It wasn't the same *him* you saw last night. The Dom who grabbed you from his apartment wasn't your Dom. Not really. He was mine."

Emily tried to understand what she was saying. "What do you mean?"

The other Emily sighed. "I'll do my best to explain. If you recall, the night Dom left you to go to the plant, there was a problem with the reactor core at Gammatech. The board was called together and they discussed what to do about the situation. It seemed there was some issue with the cooling."

"Dom said something about cooling rods acting strangely."

"They were defective. Chinese imports that Dom had ordered in an attempt to save the company money." The Emily in bed furrowed her brow. "Within a week after the night you were engaged, the reactor core went critical and suffered an explosion. It leaked radiation and caused a panic all over the plant. Luckily we were able to stop the leak before it affected the city. The safety team did an admirable job mopping up the mess and preventing a public catastrophe, but there were . . . casualties. As the new head of plant safety, I had been on scene everyday before the core went critical. And I was there the day the explosion happened. The radiation was significant. Enough to put me in the hospital for more days than not for the last few years."

Emily considered her other self in the bed. Radiation poisoning would certainly explain the changes. Her thinner hair, the spots on her skin.

"Dom blamed himself. He felt guilty for ordering the faulty rods, and he felt he never should have encouraged me to take the head of plant safety job. He believed that if I hadn't been there that day things would have been different. He didn't handle it well.

"What happened to Dom?" Emily asked.

"That's a complicated part of the story," the other Emily replied. "He hired the best doctors he could find. When it became apparent that I would need a kidney transplant, he volunteered immediately, but he wasn't a donor match. I did get a transplant but it hasn't solved my issues. My body rejected the new kidney. We even tried some of the new synthetic organs they've been experimenting with. But we had no luck. I have a kind of overactive immune system it seems, partly due to the radiation poisoning. The doctors say that my body doesn't want to accept any tissue other than my own. And without additional transplants, there's not much to be done."

Emily recalled the cooler full of ice that she knocked over in the medical facility. The doctors with the scalpel. Things were beginning to connect in her mind. "You couldn't accept tissue other than your own . . ." Her fingers tightened on the knife hidden in her sleeve.

The other Emily continued, undisturbed. "And that's why Dom

started looking at other options." She brushed some hair away from her face. "There was a period of time when I was put into a medically induced coma. They thought it would do me some good, and I think it did, but it was a dark time for Dom. We had been arguing a lot about what to do about my treatment. He wanted me to keep fighting, but I was done with it all. I had already moved out of his place and came to live here to get some space from him. But while I was in the coma, Dom searched for alternative solutions.

"I'm not sure what dark corners of the world he was looking in, but he heard rumor of a service. A service that could supply wealthy individuals with transplants. They claimed to be genetically identical tissue, guaranteed to be accepted. He liquidated almost all of his assets and paid these people to get me donor organs. He was convinced it would save me and we could still have a happy life together."

"They came for me." Emily said.

"Yes," her other self said, leveling her gaze at Emily. "I never even knew time travel existed, but when I came out of the coma, Dom was there explaining his plan to save me. He kept talking about alternate realities and a fractal universe and said that these people would be able to save me.

"At first I didn't believe him, but when he refused to back down, I did some research of my own. Historical documents, scientific journals. I began to see what he was talking about might be real. But I also realized he was talking about murder. In order to live, I'd have to end someone else's life. Your life."

Emily looked at the doorway. Carson was out of sight. Was he waiting around the corner with a weapon? Chloroform? She had been asleep in the other room. If they had meant to still harvest her organs they'd have attacked her then, wouldn't they?

She looked back to the woman in the bed.

"So what are you planning to do?" Emily asked.

"You tell me," the other Emily said. "Do you think there is a future where I cut out your organs and use them to keep me alive? What would you do?"

Emily considered the question. If roles were reversed, if she had been the one with the radiation poisoning, would she be willing to take a life? Her own life?

The woman in the bed was watching her carefully. She stared back into her eyes.

Emily relaxed her grip on the knife. She knew her answer.

Whether it was searching in her older self's eyes or somewhere in her own mind, she knew. There were things she was capable of and things she would never do. This was the latter.

The Emily in the bed smiled. "I knew you'd understand."

"I do," Emily replied.

The Emily on the bed took one of her pillows into her lap and hugged it to her chest. "There was no way I was going to agree to harvest organs from some other version of myself, no matter what reality they lived in."

"So what will you do?" Emily asked.

"I'd prefer to do nothing, and live what's left of my life in peace," the other Emily said. "But the problem is that Dom's plan has already been set in motion. He's already paid these guys to go find you. He said it was all being taken care of. I tried to convince him to cancel the deal, but he refused. He said healing me was worth every cent he had and that he would do anything to be with me forever. Even this."

Emily fidgeted with the diamond on her finger. "He's always been one for grand gestures . . ."

The door swung open and Carson came in with a tray laden with blueberry muffins and some juices. "Thought you might want a bite to eat." He smiled and set the tray on the other Emily's lap.

"I didn't know I was getting breakfast in bed with this arrangement," she replied. "If I knew that I would have called you earlier."

Carson handed her a glass of juice. "Forgot to bring a knife for the butter." He turned to Emily. "Don't happen to have one on you, do you?"

The Emily in the bed was watching her too, an amused smile playing at the corner of her mouth.

Emily reached into her sleeve and removed the knife she'd been hiding. She held it aloft for Carson.

"Thought that might have ended up in here." He winked at her as he took it. He set the knife next to the muffins, then took a napkin from the tray and stepped over to the coffee puddle on the floor.

"Oh no, let me do that!" Emily exclaimed, getting out of the chair and squatting next to him to help wipe up the spill. She rested her hand on his and he released his hold on the napkin.

"I really don't mind," he said.

"Yeah, but you weren't the klutz that spilled it," Emily replied. She couldn't help but notice the way he was looking at her. She found herself smiling as she mopped up the spill. Carson picked up the mug and stood. I'll get some cleaner for the rug if I can find some."

"There's some under the kitchen sink," the Emily in the bed replied. "But don't feel you have to. I know it's not part of your job description."

Emily stood and faced Carson. He took the soiled napkin from her hand.

"What exactly *is* your job description?" she asked.

Carson smiled and swung the napkin over his shoulder. "General knight-in-shining-armor stuff, plus occasional baking." He gestured toward the muffins. "Oh, and rock guitar." He strummed an air guitar with his right hand while fingering a chord on the coffee mug.

"Man of many talents," Emily replied.

"I thought since Dom was hiring time travelers," the other Emily said, "that I needed to go out and find one of my own. I found Carson."

Emily studied the two of them. An unusual pairing to say the least.

"So what do we do now? Is Dom still out to get me and steal my organs?"

Carson toyed with the mug. "Well, here's the thing about time travel. Some things that happen, only happen once, but some things you have to repeat."

Emily raised an eyebrow. "Repeat?"

"Sort of," Carson said. "But we need your help."

Emily chimed in from the bed, "Since Dom didn't successfully capture you for the transplant surgery, there's a chance they may try somewhere else. Possibly a different version of us."

"What do you mean? How many versions of us are there?" Emily asked.

Carson cleared his throat. "Okay, so things get a little interesting at this part, but basically time is a fractal. There can be any number of infinite timestreams to choose from. If Dom finds another version of you out there, he could potentially try again. It's most likely that he'll keep fishing around in your own collective past, because that's when he knows where to find you, but if we don't stop him, he might create another reality where you're dead or missing—the victim of these time traveling organ harvesters. We've been trying to shut this group down for a while now, but with your help, we might be able to do it."

"We? Who's we?"

"The good guys," Carson said. "People who don't want to see the time travel community ruined by rogue agents like these harvesters."

"There's a time travel community?" Emily asked.

"Yeah. One you're a part of now, even though your joining was involuntary. But with your help I think we might be able to shut these guys down."

Emily considered what he was asking. "What would I have to do?"

"We need to stop Dom."

The Emily on the bed gestured for her to come closer. When she stepped to the bedside, her other self took her hand. "I know this is a lot to ask," the other Emily said. "And I wouldn't put this on you if I was in any condition to stop him myself, but the truth is, I'm dying." She put a hand up. "I'm okay with that. I've been okay with it for quite some time. But what I'm not okay with is Dom killing someone else in my name in his misguided efforts to save me. If you can stop him, you'd be doing me a tremendous service. I think I could go peacefully if I knew that no one else had to suffer because of what happened to me. And I feel like I can ask you to do this because I know with certainty that if you were in my position, you'd feel the same way. That's the one thing I'm sure of in all this. Because you're me."

Emily rubbed a finger along the pale skin of her other self's hand. "I'm sorry this happened to you."

"You too," the other Emily replied.

Emily gently laid the woman's hand on the bed and straightened up. "Okay. I'll do it. I don't know where to start, but if it will keep more people—and more of us—from being hurt, I don't see that I have much of a choice."

The Emily in the bed nodded. "I felt the same way. I don't know exactly how to do it either, but I believe Carson has a plan. He'll help you. At least he'd better. That's what I'm paying him for." She glanced at Carson and he smiled.

"I'm on it."

Emily patted her other self's hand. "You look like you could use some rest. Thank you for rescuing me. And thank you for telling me this."

"This was my future," her other self said. "But I'm hoping it doesn't have to be yours." She gathered the edge of the comforter and pulled it a little higher on her chest. "But I'll be expecting a return visit when you're successful."

Emily nodded and followed Carson out of the room.

He led her back to the bedroom she had been asleep in previously. In the time she was gone, he had laid a pair of hard-sided suitcases on the bed.

"I brought along a few basic supplies. Typical tactical rescue stuff. But you're going to be the most essential part of this process." He opened a case to reveal an arsenal of tools, body armor, and night vision goggles.

"I am?" Emily asked. "Why?"

Carson took out a notepad and a pen from the case. "Because you're the only one who knows what to do. You've been there."

"What?"

"I'm not the one who came to your rescue when you escaped from Dom," he replied. He reached into the case and held up a black fabric ski mask. "You were."

Emily recalled the masked woman who attempted to unstrap her from the chair. The frantic eyes behind the mask. Her eyes?

"Why do I feel like my life has never been this complicated," Emily said. "Is this what yours is like all the time?"

Carson smiled and tossed her the mask. "Welcome to time travel."

6

"You said there was a flash and then the lights went out. Maybe some kind of flash bang grenade?" Carson asked. "What other details can you remember?"

Emily brushed her hair back from her face with both hands. "Just what I've told you already. It was pretty hard to see once they had that shower curtain thing around me. They had me on some kind of IV too. It was all a little fuzzy."

"Sounds like a portable gravitizer. A rush job."

"There you go making up words again," Emily said.

Carson set his pen down on the table. They were back outside sharing one side of the patio table and letting the afternoon sun warm their backs.

"I think I've got the basic picture. They had to treat you with gravitites—they are these particles that enable your body and clothing to make the transition through the time gate. The external treatment would have worked fine for your clothes and your major bits and pieces, but they would've wanted to make sure you had a good amount of gravitites all through your body to make sure nothing got left behind in the jump."

"Left behind?"

"Yeah. You remember the handcuffs?" He pulled the metal flashlight-looking device from his pocket. "I used this to remove the gravitite particles in a section of the cuffs so that when I jumped us forward a couple of seconds those bits got left behind. You wouldn't want that to happen with your body though. And they wouldn't either, considering they wanted to make use of your organs over here."

Emily was still struggling to process all that he had told her today. "So I'm really in a totally alternate reality right now . . ." She looked up to the city around her. The skyline looked mostly the same if you didn't count the sign on the former Gammatech building. Citizens were just going about their normal days down on the street.

"I know it's strange to think about, but everyone you see down there thinks this is all there is," Carson said. "All of reality. Truth is that there are lots of realities. We call them timestreams. But there is only one that you come from. Goal is to get you back there, minus the organ snatching scumbags."

"And we have to get it just right? What happens if we mess it up?" Emily asked.

"I'm not worried about every single detail, those tend to take care of themselves more often than not, but if we alter what happened too drastically, there's a chance the universe pitches a fit and the timestream itself starts to fracture. We might create a new timestream and create a whole new set of problems with it. But try not to worry about that. Most times, when you go back in time to a place you've already been, you're going to act naturally. So past, er, future you in this case, will behave just like you already did in your memory. Try not to overthink it."

"That's like saying 'don't think about pink elephants.' The more I try not to worry, the more I find to worry about."

Carson smiled. "Yeah, well, just do the best you can. And we'll try to avoid all proverbial elephants, no matter the color."

"When are we doing this?" Emily asked.

"The sooner the better, I guess," Carson said. "With my research on these guys I knew where the facility was on our end, but from what you said, we'll be hitting them on your side of the time gate."

"But I already know we fail," Emily said. "I don't get myself untied and Axle shoves me through the gate thingy. If I can't rescue me, then how do we stop them?"

"The mission here isn't to rescue you. But you do need to get in and untie the straps on the chair. From what you said, that was a key to your escape once you were over here. The rest should take care of itself. Once your earlier self is through the gate, we need to stop Dom and shut down their operation. If I can destroy their time gate on that end, they won't have any way back to your timestream. Axle will be stuck there and we can bring him to the authorities."

"He won't time travel away?"

"These harvesters operate outside the law and under the time travel radar so to speak. They won't have wrist mounted chronometers like mine and any other portable tech they could steal wouldn't work without the time travel authorities being able to track them. That time gate is their meal ticket. I don't know who they jacked it from, but I doubt they have more than one. Not this bunch anyway. I know their methods. We get in and bust it up, I can handle them. You just need to deal with Dom. Sounds like he's a pretty desperate character right now."

Emily twisted the engagement ring on her finger, then looked toward the interior of the condo. "All right, then let's get it over with. It doesn't seem like Emily has a lot longer to wait."

Carson nodded. "Okay. Let's suit up."

Emily dressed in more of her other self's clothes that Carson had treated with the special gravitite particles for her. He'd chosen her a long-sleeved black shirt that would be comfortable under the body armor. Heavy lace-up boots and leather gloves complemented the black balaclava he had already given her. She had never worn a ski mask like it before and found it odd to have so much of her face covered, but it was also vaguely comforting knowing no one would know her identity. It was a vast improvement over her attire from the night before and she felt more confident about facing Axle and his cronies now that she wasn't half-naked and intoxicated. She rolled the ski mask up on her head to resemble a beanie and joined Carson in the living room.

"Did these guys have guns?" Carson asked as she approached the table.

"Not that I remember," Emily replied.

"Good. Makes sense they wouldn't have needed one. Wouldn't be logical to shoot you if they wanted you alive for the crossing."

"Do we have weapons?" Emily asked.

Carson held up his wrist and displayed the chronometer on it. "Got the only one we need right here."

Emily nodded. She still felt nervous about confronting Dom, knowing now what his real plan for her had been—but she would deal with that issue when she came to it. First she had to concentrate on the next hurdle in their plan. The 'minor' problem of exiting the world as she knew it and time traveling to an alternate reality.

"Should we say goodbye to Emily?" She asked as Carson finished gathering their things.

"I just checked on her," he replied. "She's asleep. But I've got anchors from here when we want to jump back. Don't worry. We won't be gone long."

"If you say so," Emily replied.

Carson asked her to place her hand on his shoulder again while he pressed a finger to a little metal disc with a hole in the middle. He put his other hand on his wrist-mounted chronometer.

"You ready?" Carson asked.

She took a deep breath and nodded.

"Okay, three, two, one—"

The world blinked again.

This time Emily found herself somewhere completely new. Carson still had his fingers on the little metal disc, but in this location it was actually a washer being used to fasten bolted-on iron bars on the windowsill of an alley window. A dumpster stood a few feet away and the wall was covered in graffiti.

"Wow," Emily said. "That was incredible!"

Carson pulled a phone from his pocket, located a picture of the washer on the windowsill and deleted it.

"What are you doing that for?" Emily asked.

"You never want to use the same anchor spot twice. At least not at the same time. You can fuse yourself with another version of you and die. Come on, we need to leave. My younger self is waiting around that corner and is going to come unbolt this washer in a few minutes. We don't want to run into him."

"There's another you here?"

"Yeah," Carson said, grabbing her arm and leading her in the opposite direction of the corner he pointed to. "I jumped ahead from this morning to set up the anchor location. I figured we'd need it."

"You set it up before Emily even asked me to do this?" Emily said.

"She seemed confident you'd agree," Carson replied. "Looks like she was right."

Once they turned the corner Carson paused to unfasten his bag.

"Can I look?" Emily asked. "Just to see him?"

Carson considered her request. "Only if you're super careful. He can't see you."

Emily stepped back to the corner and very cautiously leaned toward the edge of the brick wall, peeking around the corner with one eye.

Sure enough, there was another Carson walking up to the barred window they had just left carrying a socket wrench and a phone. He stopped to take a picture of the window. Emily put her hand over her mouth and ducked back behind the cover of the wall. "That's crazy," she whispered.

"Come on. Action time," Carson replied. He pulled his mask over his face and Emily followed suit.

They walked around the block and Emily found herself facing the back parking lot of the Gammatech research facility. Carson walked confidently across the street while carrying a bolt-cutter from his bag. He clipped his way through the chain link fence with clean, efficient movements, then pulled a section of fence open for Emily to enter. "Hurry," he said. "Security guard will walk by in about ninety seconds."

Emily hustled through the hole in the fence and Carson followed, leading her to yet another dumpster and ducking behind it. They waited silently as a man walked around the corner of the building. In all black sitting in the shadow of the building, Emily knew they would be difficult to see, but he might have a flashlight.

It turned out the security guard was on his phone. He walked by their location but never once looked at the fence or the dumpster area. He just drifted by, engrossed by the screen in his hand. Emily recognized him in the glow of his device. She was pretty sure he used to work in her building. He wouldn't for long if this was how he guarded all the time. She'd have to put in an email to the head of security on Monday . . .

"Coast should be clear. But keep an eye out." Carson moved to a metal door on the building and pulled a pair of small tools from his pocket. He inserted an L shaped bit of metal into the lock, then used a thin pick to engage the pins inside. Emily scanned the parking lot and fence as he worked, but there was no sign of security. Perhaps thirty seconds later, Carson had the door open.

"Another talent on your list?" Emily asked.

Carson pulled his mask up. His eyes were bright and he smiled.

He led her at a quick pace to an intersection of hallways. "You remember which room you were in?" he asked. He let Emily go ahead and she scanned the hallways.

Emily rolled her mask up and pointed. "That way. The one on the end."

When they reached the door, Carson extended a hand toward the doorknob, ready to insert his lock picking tools again.

"Wait," Emily whispered. "That won't work. Dom had a chain and padlock on this door. I remember he moved it inside when we went in. I know the combination, but it's on the wrong side of the door."

"Damn," Carson muttered. "That makes things more complicated. Any other doors?"

"Not that I saw. Just a window, but we definitely didn't get in that way."

Carson considered the closed door. "Well, there's one more thing I could try. A trick a friend of mine recently taught me." He fished in his bag and found a compact disk case and extracted a CD. The kind people used to play music on around the turn of the century.

"Where on earth did you find that?" Emily asked.

"It's Abbey Road. You don't have this album?"

"Not on CD. You live in 1990 or something?"

Carson got down on one knee. "I'm from 2009 actually. You'd like it. We still have Michael Jackson there." He got all the way to the floor and looked under the door. He tested the space under the door with the CD. "I think this will work." He laid the CD on the floor of the hallway, pulled out his degravitizer, and proceeded to run it across it the way he had done with the handcuffs. This time he did all of it. A light on the tool turned green and he stood back up. "Come on. We need to go back outside. Or at least around the corner." He jerked his head toward the intersection of hallways. "Time to pull a Ben."

"He's the one who taught you this?"

"Yeah, total asshole. Likes to have all the fun without me."

Emily followed Carson around the corner and he pulled a phone from his pocket. He set the timer on it for thirty seconds. They waited quietly, and when the thirty seconds were expired, they went back around the corner. Emily was surprised to find that the disc on the floor was just as they'd left it. Nothing had changed or disintegrated. But Carson got back on the floor again, and this time he flicked the Beatles CD under the door. When he straightened up, he indicated for her to grab hold of him. He dialed something on his chronometer. "We're going to make two jumps, one to thirty seconds ago in this hallway, and then another forward to the other side of this door where the CD is now. Don't make any sounds till we're on the other side, okay?"

Emily nodded.

Carson quickly handed her a flash bang grenade from his bag. "And you can hold this." He also handed her a pair of earplugs to put in. "And be sure to close your eyes when we lob this thing."

Emily put her earplugs in and nodded, then rolled the mask back over her face. Carson did the same.

He put his hand to the wall, then pressed a pin on his chronometer with his other hand. They blinked.

The hallway looked exactly the same except the CD was back on the floor near their feet. Carson put a finger to his lips, then squatted down to touch the CD this time. "Get ready," he mouthed. She took a firm grip on his shoulder. He dialed his chronometer settings again for a forward direction and pressed the pin.

They were inside.

Emily looked up from where they arrived, crouched over the CD on the floor, and found herself back in the room with racks of electronics. Dom and Axle were stooped over a control monitor near the strange opaque curtain. The hazy shape of a person in a chair was visible through the material. The multi-colored doorway stood at the far side of the room, still just as mesmerizing and beautiful as it was the first time.

"Did it work? Did she receive enough?" Dom asked.

"Should be plenty," Axle replied. Neither of them was looking toward the entrance.

Carson took the flash bang grenade from her hand, pulled the pin and lobbed it.

Then he turned toward her, closed his eyes, and covered his ears. Emily did the same.

The boom was significant and she could see the brilliance of the light even with her eyes closed. When she opened them Carson was already reaching for the light switch by the door.

The next moment the room went dark. The only remaining light was the swirling brilliance of the door through time.

7

C arson was on the move.

Emily watched his dark shape sprint toward Dom and Axle, then tackle Axle to the ground.

Axle shouted as Carson hit him, then collided with the side of the gravitizer curtain as he fell.

Carson looked her direction as he grappled with the man, who was attempting to draw a knife. The knife.

She'd forgotten to tell Carson about the knife!

Carson shouted. "Get her loose!"

Emily came unfrozen and ran for the framework of tubing.

Dom was still rubbing his eyes and trying to regain his senses from the blast. She skirted him and ducked inside the portable gravitizer with her earlier self.

The other her in the chair was blinking and disoriented. Emily reached for the straps on the chair arms and began tearing the Velcro loose.

"Dom?" her other self asked.

Emily positioned herself in front of her as she loosened the other strap. "Listen, you have to run!"

Her other self looked baffled but seemed to understand.

"No! Don't touch her!" Dom shouted as he flung the tubular framework aside and grabbed for her. Emily backed away as he pursued her, his fist raised.

She held up her hands, backpedaling. What was she supposed to do now?

She searched for Carson. His shape was on the floor where he'd been wrestling with Axle. There was a smear on the floor. Blood?

Axle was at the chair now, shoving her earlier self toward the door. "Have a nice trip!"

Dom turned in time to see the other Emily go flying toward the multicolored doorway. "No, wait!" he shouted.

Axle had already released her, however, and the other Emily went rolling through the doorway and disappeared.

The colors in the doorway flared brighter for a moment, then Axle turned and leered at her. "And who have we got here?"

Dom focused his attention on her as well.

She was trapped. Racks of old electronics blocked her on one side and the two men were closing in on her. "Your meddling is going to cost you," Dom said, raising a fist to strike her.

"No! Dom, it's me!" Emily reached up and yanked the mask from her head. Her hair fell around her face and she held her other hand up.

"Emily?" Dom's fist wavered, then fell to his side. "What on earth?" He glanced back at the time gate, then to Axle.

Axle narrowed his eyes, then pulled the knife from his belt. "You didn't say there were spares, mack. You want to slice and dice this one too?"

"I know what happened, Dom," Emily said. "I met your Emily. She doesn't want you to do this."

Dom's expression turned into a scowl. "You're trying to stop me from saving her. You don't know anything."

"I know that if you love her, if you love me, you won't hurt anyone. It's not too late to stop this."

51

"Wait a minute," Axle muttered. "Just where did you come from?" He glanced back at the time gate. "What did you do?"

"Your men on the other side clearly weren't as efficient as advertised," Dom growled. "And you still need to finish the job." Dom backed up, leaving room for Axle to get to her.

Axle brandished the knife. "Maybe we'll try taking her through in pieces this time . . ."

"No, Dom. Don't do this," Emily pleaded as he continued to back away. "You don't want to hurt me. I know you don't."

"I told you, Emily. I would do anything to keep you. Anything."

Axle reached for her and she screamed.

Suddenly the room went completely dark. The brilliance of the time gate was gone.

Axle cursed. Something crashed to the floor on the far side of the room and smashed.

Emily couldn't see anything but she ran, feeling her way past the nearest rack of shelves and making for the wall with the exit door.

"What did you do?" Axle screamed, crashing into something on the other side of the room. "I thought I gutted your ass."

Emily scrambled along the wall, feeling for the door, till she found the handle. She swore when she felt the chain locking it. She felt for the padlock. She knew the combination but she couldn't see it. She reached for the light switch next to the door.

As the fluorescent overhead lights flickered to life, they revealed the chaos of the room. Equipment lay strewn across the floor from where she'd collided with it. The gravitizer curtain was in a heap, and the space formerly occupied by the time gate was now bare. Carson had ripped the frame down and dismembered the control box. He was standing among the fragments and bundles of wiring lay in piles around his feet. His left arm was bloody, but he shouted to her across the room. "Go! I got this!"

Emily entered her birthday into the lock and pulled it free. That's when she saw Dom heading for her. She pulled the chain loose from the door and hurled it at him. Dom ducked but the chain struck him anyway, causing him to stagger back. Emily flung the door open and raced into the hall.

When she reached the intersection, she struggled to remember which way they came in. She went right. Sprinting down the hallway, she quickly realized she had made the wrong choice. There was no exit door here, just an elevator and a door to a stairwell.

Dom rounded the corner just as she turned around. He wasn't running, but he strode steadily forward, a cut bleeding above his right eye. He was carrying the chain.

Emily jammed her finger against the elevator button, but as it illuminated she quickly realized she wouldn't have enough time. She spun and pushed through the doors to the stairwell.

There was no exit here either. Just the steps climbing up. She sprinted up them to the next landing.

The door to the first floor was locked. She rattled the handle but it refused to open. Swearing, she took the steps two at a time to the next landing. The door was locked there as well. She leaned over the railing and looked down. Dom was climbing. Not running, but making steady progress up the stairs, the chain jingling as he walked. He looked up and glared at her, his features unsympathetic.

Emily climbed to the next floor, and then the next. At the fifth floor the signage finally changed, indicating that the next level was the roof. Emily prayed that someone had heeded a fire marshal and at least left that door unlocked. When she reached the top of the stairs, she pressed on the door and was relieved to feel it swing open. She stepped onto the roof and slowly spun around.

There was no elevator up here. It didn't come up this high. No way back down.

She worked to catch her breath as she scoured the roof for a place to hide. A number of industrial air conditioning units were scattered along the roof, but there was nowhere she wouldn't be easily seen. She found one that was still relatively close to the stairs but a little to the side. If Dom went a different direction at first, perhaps she could race back down the stairs and escape.

She crouched behind the air conditioner and waited.

A few moments later the door swung open. Light from the stairwell spilled onto the roof. Dom's shadow stretched across the gravel and tar paper. He waited for a few seconds, then stepped onto the roof.

"There's nowhere to run, Emily," he called out. He walked a few steps but then turned and closed the door. To Emily's dismay, he fished the chain through the door handle and secured it to a drainpipe next to the door. It wasn't locked, but he managed to knot it.

There would be no easy escape that way. He would be sure to catch her the moment she reached the door. Perhaps if he got far enough away?

"You don't understand, Emily," Dom said, scanning the rooftop. "I'm doing this for us. So that we can be together." He took a few steps forward. "I've come to understand that there's nothing else that matters in this life. Not work. Not family. It's who we *choose* to love that matters."

He walked around the first of the air conditioner units and paused, surveying the roof behind him.

"When Gammatech suffered that explosion, it was my fault. I know that now. I should have listened to the inspectors. I should have shut down the plant as soon as I heard about the problem. But I was arrogant. I thought that I knew the system better than they did. I was sure that my new cooling rods could take the strain."

He took a few more steps and angled toward the next air conditioner. He was getting closer.

"What happened to you was my fault, Emily. That's why I have to fix it. You're the only thing that I ever got right. After all that's happened. With Gammatech, with my father, none of it was ever what mattered. But I had you. And that's what I'm going to do with the rest of my life. Live to make you happy."

He checked behind the air conditioner nearest to him and then proceeded to the next one—the one Emily was hiding behind. "I know you've been gone, Emily. I know you don't see it like I do and that's why you left me. But you're sick. Once you're healthy again, then you'll see. Then you'll remember why you love me. That will be my gift to you."

Emily stood up and revealed herself. She stepped back to keep the air conditioning unit between her and Dom. "She doesn't want this, Dom. This won't make her happy. It won't make her want you back."

Dom studied her, determination in his eyes. He edged his way closer. "You're wrong. You just don't see. You're sick. Once you're better—"

"You're confused, Dom. I'm not her." Emily said. "She's had five years to make her decision and she's made it. There's nothing you can do to change her mind." She sidestepped to keep him at a distance on the other side of the equipment. He continued to edge around it.

"You're mine," Dom said. "Even when all else was going wrong, I still had you. You are my everything. All I have left."

"I don't want to be your everything," Emily replied. "If there is anything I've learned in the last 24 hours, it's that. What you're doing isn't love. It's obsession."

Dom's expression turned into a scowl. "You don't know what I've been through."

"And I don't plan to find out," Emily muttered. Dom had made it far enough around the air conditioner that she had a line to the stairs. She turned and sprinted for the door.

Dom rushed to pursue her.

Emily's boots pounded across the roof as she ran, arms pumping, but Dom was too fast. She looked back to see him almost on top of her. She wouldn't make it in time to free the chain. She veered left and ran for the cover of another air conditioning unit towards the edge of the roof. But this one had a lower profile. As soon as she got beyond it, Dom leapt and landed atop it, looming over her.

Emily gasped and tried to run around, but Dom hurled himself down at her, tackling her to the rooftop. She flailed in his arms, elbowing him in the gut and trying to scramble away, but he grabbed her boot and tripped her up. She managed to get to her feet and spin around, but she was trapped, stuck at the corner of the roof with no way down. It was a six story drop to the asphalt parking lot.

"You've got nowhere to run," Dom said.

Emily glared at him. "Neither do you, Dom. Your way back to your time is broken. We've seen to that."

Dom reached for her arms. She tried to avoid him but there was nowhere to go. He grabbed her wrists.

"I'll find a way. I can still save you. I'll save us." He pulled her closer to him, his face inches from hers. "There's nothing I wouldn't do to keep you," he said.

Emily clenched her fists and went rigid in his grip. "There's nothing left to do. Even if you found a way back, she's dying, Dom. She's leaving you. It's what she wants."

Dom searched her face, looking for the truth of what she was saying. "*You* came back. You still love me. It's why you are here."

"I don't, Dom. I did before, but not the man you've become. I came back to stop you. To keep you from hurting anyone else."

"I didn't do this to hurt you!" Dom screamed in her face. "I would never hurt you. Never!" He was shaking with rage.

Emily cringed in his grip. "You're doing it right now, Dom. You're hurting me."

Dom looked at his hands and the way her wrists were turning purple in his grip, then he turned and threw her to the rooftop. She crunched into the tar paper in a heap. She rubbed her wrists. When Emily looked up, Dom was looking at his own shaking hands. He ran them over his head and backed away a few steps. When he finally looked at her, the rage seemed to be subsiding.

"I spent the last of what I had to save you. Gammatech . . . my inheritance—it's all gone now. But I'd do it again. I would have given anything," he said. "just to share a lifetime with you." He took another step backward, his heel now at the edge of the roof.

"You had one lifetime of mine," Emily replied, slowly climbing to her feet. "That's all you get."

Dom stared at her in defeat, his features slowly relaxing. "You're right. You're not her. You won't ever understand." He lifted his eyes skyward. "There's only one way left to be with my Emily now." He spread his arms and took a step backward.

"Dom, no! Wait!" Emily reached out a hand, but he was tipping over backward, arms wide, till he tumbled headfirst over the edge.

Emily took a step forward but then stopped when she heard the sound of him hitting the asphalt below.

She sank to her knees.

8

"There was nothing you could have done," Carson said.

Emily wasn't sure how long she had sat on the roof before he found her, but he did. He knelt next to her and put a hand on her back. He waited like that till she was ready to move, then helped her up. She didn't look over the edge, just turned and headed for the stairs.

"What happened to Axle?" Emily asked. "Are we safe?"

"He's tied to a drain pipe downstairs. I've already alerted the time travel authorities to his location. They'll pick him up."

Emily put a hand on Carson's arm. His shirt was cut in multiple places and his shoulder had been hastily bandaged.

"I thought you were dead when I saw you on the floor. I forgot to tell you about the knife . . ."

Carson pulled his ripped shirt open to reveal the body armor covering his chest. "When in doubt, go with the stab-proof vest."

"I'm sorry if I put you in added danger."

Carson shook his head. "You're the one who had to handle Dom on your own. I owe you an apology for that."

"So, there are some things even time travelers can't plan for?" she asked.

"We're rewriting the story now. All new possibilities."

Emily wrapped her arms across her chest. "What do we have to do next? Is it over?"

"The time gate is shut down. We've stopped the immediate threat to other versions of yourself out there in the multiverse. But it's never over till you report back to the boss," Carson replied. "I think we need to pay her a visit."

Emily nodded. "I'm glad we're going back. I have a few questions for her."

The return jump to the condo in Highland Park was instantaneous, once Carson degravitized an anchor from there. One of the dresser drawers would now be missing a knob, after Carson's earlier self showed up to borrow it, but Emily imagined her future self wouldn't mind.

The other Emily stirred in her bed when they entered the bedroom. She had a far-off look in her eyes but she focused on Emily when she sat down next to her.

"You did it."

Emily nodded. "Dom won't be hurting anyone else. At least not from this time."

"You must have had a difficult time," her other self said. "I can't imagine living through the kind of day you've had."

"It's been eye-opening," Emily replied. "I can say that much." She fidgeted with the ring on her finger. "When did you first know? About Dom. When did you know you had to leave him?"

"I think I always knew. That's why we never went through with it. I moved into his place after the engagement, but never had the wedding. Once I got sick, everything was different. I don't think I was surprised though. Dom had always had that intensity about him. I suppose he really did love me. But there are some things that even love can't fix."

Emily nodded.

"You'll have some difficult decisions to make when you get home," the other Emily said. "All of this is still a possible future for you there, unless you do something about it."

"I plan to make sure things go differently."

The other Emily gestured to Carson. "In my desk there, top drawer. There's a communications card. My contact at the Federal Energy Commission. She's a good woman. She'll listen if you report the danger at the plant."

Carson found the card and handed it to Emily.

"And who knows," the other Emily continued. "Perhaps they are looking for more agents. They could use someone with our background."

"Thanks," Emily replied. "I'll give her a call." She looked at the woman in the bed. She was even more frail than the last time she saw her, but she seemed relaxed now. Nothing weighing on her. "Is there anything else I can do for you? Do you need help with . . ." She trailed off.

"With dying?" her other self replied. She smiled. "Just come hold my hand for a few minutes. Then, when you're ready, go live the life we both want. You can finish it for the both of us."

Emily moved her chair forward and took her other self's hand. "I don't think I know what future I want anymore."

Her other self smiled. "And that will be the best part."

9

The elevator dinged when the doors opened. Emily stepped into Dom's penthouse and looked around. The bottle of champagne was still dripping beads of condensation onto the countertop.

"Welcome back, Miss Davis," Avery said.

Emily ignored her and headed for the bathroom. She looked herself in the mirror, focused on her own reflection, and breathed out. "You can do this."

She was no longer wearing body armor, but her reflection still looked confident.

She reached into the tub and manually pulled the drain for the lavender and tea tree scented bath. The water was still warm.

When she straightened up, she addressed Avery. "Where's Dom?"

"Mr. Del Toro is en route from Gammatech via his personal vehicle. Would you like me to contact him?"

"No. I'll wait."

Emily strode back into the dining room, pulled the engagement ring from her finger, and set it on the countertop next to the champagne bottle. She took off her jacket.

Then she waited.

Dom slipped through the door about a quarter of an hour before midnight. He had loosened his tie and looked worried, but his smile brightened when he saw her sitting in the armchair in the living room.

"You're still up. I'm glad. I'm sorry that took so long. Inspectors were all in a tizzy and I had to calm them down. They worry like hens over the slightest thing."

"The defective cooling rods," Emily said.

"Yes. I mean no," Dom said, eyeing her outfit and boots. "There's nothing wrong with them. I ordered them myself, at a significant discount. The indications are a little off from our normal parameters, but the new rods are every bit as good as the ones we had before. The inspectors just needed a little convincing. They've agreed to let it go for the time being."

"The federal inspectors aren't going to see it that way," Emily replied. "I think you'll want to shut operations down and ensure the safety of the facility first thing in the morning. They'll want to see you in full emergency management mode when they arrive. It's the best hope for the company."

"Feds? No. There aren't any federal inspectors involved. It was just our people. They're all on board with me now."

"Your new head of plant safety isn't," Emily said. "Shouldn't you have consulted her first?"

Dom smiled and moved toward her. "Last I saw, my head of plant safety was three sheets to the wind and not wearing any pants. Just the way I like her . . ." He began to reach for her.

Emily lifted her leg and planted her boot on Dom's belt buckle, keeping him at a distance. "I already spoke with them. The federal inspectors. They'll be here in the morning."

"What?" Dom backed up a step. "What are you talking about? You don't even know what's going on, and it's the middle of the night. No agency is going to take your call right now. Not in this town."

"You don't understand, Dom. I've been to tomorrow. It's done." Emily stood and moved to the counter.

Dom studied her face. "You're not making sense."

"I just came back for one reason," Emily said. "Because I think that there is still a chance for you. If you make the right decisions now, you can save yourself, and the company."

"How much have you had to drink while I was gone?" Dom asked. "Why don't we just forget about this conversation for now. We can head back to the bedroom and celebrate—" His eyes fell on the ring sitting next to the champagne bottle. He turned and appraised her more seriously. "What's really going on here? You're mad I left for the meeting? You think I should have stayed."

"No, Dom. For once, this isn't about me at all. It's all about you. What's best for you."

"Emily, honey. Just tell me what you really want. You know I love you. I'd do anything for you. Anything."

"I know, Dom. I don't just believe you when you say that, I know it's true. But if you love me, if you respect me, you'll do this. You'll shut the plant down tomorrow. You'll spend the money and replace the defective rods. You'll do the right thing. The company will have losses in the short term, but they are losses you'll be able to live with. Gammatech will survive. And so will you."

Dom picked up the ring and held it in his fingertips. "And you'll stay?"

Emily picked up her jacket and strode toward the opening elevator.

"Emily?" Dom pivoted on his heel to follow her, incredulous.

When Emily stepped into the elevator and turned around, she finally addressed him calmly. "Goodbye, Dom. I know you won't believe this right away, but I'm hoping you will one day." The elevator doors began to close. "Trust that I know how this ends, and you'll have a better future without me."

1 0

W hen the public car pulled up to the curb in front of her building, Emily hesitated. But this time things looked correct. She could feel it.

She climbed out of the car and stared up at the starry sky. The clouds had cleared.

No. That wasn't it. They hadn't been made yet, like the rest of her future.

The automatic lighting illuminated her path as she climbed the steps to the front door. The fingerprint pad greeted her with its amber glow. She raised her thumb to press down and unlock the door, but hesitated.

"This *is* my house this time, right?" She turned around and faced the red-headed man who had appeared on the sidewalk.

"Do you want it to be?" Carson asked.

Emily smiled at him. "Are there other options?"

He was grinning back at her. "I can think of a few million or so. Universe is full of possibilities." Carson's grin slowly faded. "How did it go tonight?"

Emily put her hands in her jacket pockets. "Well, I was able to end an engagement and tender my resignation in the same night. So, I guess I get points for efficiency."

"Sounds like good time management to me," Carson said. "That's a valuable skill."

"You would know, I guess," Emily said. "What's next for you? More knight-in-shining-armor stuff? Another damsel in distress to save somewhere? Or is it some-when?"

Carson stared up at the stars for a moment. "I suppose there might be more out there, but I've been thinking I'd like to spend a little time working on my other skills too. Gotta keep things fresh. Don't want life to get repetitive. I feel like it's my duty to change things up."

"That's too bad," Emily said. "I was kind of hoping you stopped by to make me some of those blueberry muffins. They smelled delicious."

Carson rocked back and forth on his heels. "Hmm. It seems we're at a difficult junction then. Past and future on the line once again. Whatever will we do?"

Emily studied his laughing blue eyes. Despite the chaos of her recent past and the mystery of her unknown future, the night seemed suddenly full of intriguing possibilities.

"I have eggs," she offered. "How are you at making omelettes?"

Carson considered her, then smiled again. "You know, that's a breakfast I've always wanted to master." He climbed the steps to join her.

Emily smiled and unlocked the door.

IN TIMES LIKE THESE

"Don't assume that because you know something in the future won't happen, that you can do nothing. Sometimes the reason it doesn't happen is you."
-Excerpt from the journal of Dr. Harold Quickly, 1997

I have far too much of my life in my arms to even think of reaching for my phone when it starts ringing in my pocket. I concentrate on getting the key in the lock. That and not dropping the shoes, water bottles and mail I've hauled to the door of my apartment. I get the door open with my free fingers and just make it inside when one of the water bottles escapes. The next moment, all but my useless junk mail is on the living room floor. I leave it there and open my phone the moment before it gives up on me.

"Hey, Carson. What's up?"

"Dude. You coming to batting practice?"

"Yeah, I'll be there. Just got home from work."

"Okay, can you check the weather while you're there?"

"No problem. Be there in a few."

I toss my phone and the junk mail onto the couch and locate the remote in the cushions. The station is still on commercials, so I head for the kitchen. Depositing the remote on the counter, I turn to the refrigerator out of habit. It's still just as sparse as the last time I checked. I settle for my one remaining bottle of water and head for the bedroom to change. The news broadcast comes on from around the corner.

"Welcome back to News Channel 8. In a few moments we'll get your Drive Time Traffic and weather, but first, a look at today's top stories.

"Today was the conclusion of the eight month trial of Elton Stenger, the man accused of murdering fourteen people in a series of vicious car bombings and shootings throughout the state of Florida. Judge Alan Waters ruled today that Stenger be convicted, and serve fourteen consecutive life sentences, a record number for the state of Florida. Stenger is being transported today into federal custody and will be tried in the state of New York for three additional murders."

I pull my paycheck from my shorts pocket and lay it on the dresser. It'll be gone in a week. Emptying the meager contents of my wallet out next to the check, I extract enough cash for a couple of post-game beers. *Minimal celebrating is still better than no celebrating.*

"Today is a monumental day for St. Petersburg and the entire scientific community, as the St. Petersburg Temporal Studies Society gets set to test their latest particle accelerator, what they claim may be the world's first time machine. They will attempt to launch a number of particles through time and space in their laboratory here in St. Petersburg today.

"We have correspondent David Powers on the scene. David, what's going on down there?"

I get into my athletic shorts and snag some socks. *Where the hell did I put my uniform shirt?* I cruise through the living room to head for my laundry closet.

" . . . and while the potential applications of the experiment are yet to be determined, one thing is for certain, these researchers won't be wasting any time. Back to you, Barbara."

I glimpse the blonde woman grinning on screen with her co-anchor. "Next thing we know they'll be rolling out a Delorean. Certainly a day to remember. Now we go to Carl Sims with our weather update."

I know what it's going to say. Hot. Chance of thunderstorms. This is Florida. I locate my wrinkled *Hit Storm* shirt in the laundry basket, and slide it over my head as I walk back around the corner to the TV. Just as expected, the little cloud and lightning symbol dominates the entire week.

When I arrive at the field, most of the team is already there. I spot Carson's orange hair as he's out on the mound throwing batting practice. As I step out of my car, the moist, sweet smell of clay and grass clippings makes my shoulders instantly relax. Each step I take toward the field helps the tension of my workday ebb away. Robbie is donning his cleats in the dugout as I walk up.

"Hey, man." I throw my glove into the cubby beside his.

"What's up, Ben? How's it going?"

"Hoping we're going to get to play this one," I reply.

"Yeah me too, I'm going to forget how to swing a bat if we keep getting rained out." Robbie stands and stretches his arms toward the roof of the dugout. My arms would reach it. At 5'8" Robbie's come up short. What he lacks in height he makes up for in fitness. Despite his on again, off again cigarette habit, he can still out-sprint anyone on the team. His lean and muscular physique is contrasted by his relaxed demeanor; a constant state of ease that makes me feel like I'm rushing through life by comparison.

"Have we got enough people tonight? I know Nick said he was going to be out of town in Georgia or something like that." I kick off my flip-flops and start pulling on a sock.

"Yeah, I think Blake's going to second and Mike's filling in at catcher. We should be good. There's Blake now." Robbie gestures with his head while he leans forward and stretches his arms behind his back.

Blake's Jeep pulls into the space next to my truck. I'm happy I'm not the only one who has missed most of practice. Blake and I have a lot in common, including our propensity for arriving fashionably late. Blake's my height, and while his hair borders on black compared to my brown, we occasionally get mistaken for brothers.

"You wanna throw?" Robbie asks, as I finish lacing up.

"Yeah." I grab my glove and the two of us toss the ball along the sideline until Blake joins us.

"Is Mallory making it out to the game tonight?" I ask Blake as he lines up next to me.

He stretches his right arm across his chest and then switches to the other one. "I doubt it. She has to watch her niece and I don't think she wants to bring her out."

We never get many fans at our games. Blake's girlfriend is the most frequent but even her appearances have gotten rare. I keep inviting people, but apparently Wednesday nights are more highly valued elsewhere. *Can't remember the last time a girlfriend of mine made it out to a game. Three seasons ago? Four? I suppose managing to keep one longer than a few months might help.*

Carson pitches us each a bucket of softballs, and I knock the majority of mine toward an increasingly dark right field. We ignore the clouds as much as possible and concentrate on practice. Once everyone has hit, we mill around the dugout, stretching, while Carson gives me his appraisal of our chances.

"These guys should be cake for us. I watched them play last week. I think we're going to crush 'em."

I consider the big athletic guys filling the opposing dugout and realize that Carson might be overly optimistic, but I don't argue. "We're definitely due for a win."

Carson starts jotting down the lineup. He's full of energy today. I admire that about him. At twenty-five, he's a little younger than me, but about a year older than Blake. He has no trouble organizing things like this. Sports are his arena. He's naturally talented at all of them. I could outrun him. Blake could outswim us both, but Carson has everybody beat on all-around athleticism. He makes a great shortstop in any case. The other teams have learned to fear both his fielding abilities and his trash talking skills. Blake and I flank him on the field at second and third base respectively.

We walk out to our positions and are waiting for Robbie to throw the first pitch, when a thunderclap rumbles through the clouds. The umpire casts a quick glance skyward, but then yells, "Batter Up!"

I'm digging my cleats into the dirt at third when I notice my friend Francesca walking up from the parking lot. She catches my eye and sticks her tongue out at me before sitting down next to Paul, our designated hitter. I scowl at her and she laughs, and then turns to greet Paul. *What do you know? We did manage a fan tonight.*

The crack of the bat jerks my attention back to the game as the ground ball takes a bad hop a few feet in front of me and impacts me in the chest. It drops to the ground and I scramble to bare hand it, making the throw to first just a step ahead of the runner. I rub my chest as I walk back to my position. *That'll be a bruise tomorrow.*

Robbie walks the next batter as I start to feel the first few drops of rain. The third batter grounds to Blake at second. He underhand tosses the ball to Carson who tags the base and hurls it to first for a double play, just as a bolt of lightning flashes beyond right field. Carson's yell of success over the play is drowned out by the boom of thunder. I head for the dugout, hoping we'll get a chance to hit, but as the outfielders come trotting in, they're followed by a dense wall of rain. I step into the dugout before the heavy drops can soak me.

"Hey Fresca, What's shakin'?" I plop down next to Francesca on the bench.

"I finally make it to one of your games and this is how you treat me?" She gestures to the sheets of rain now sweeping the field.

"I ordered you sunshine and double rainbows, but they must not have gotten the memo."

"I was worried I was going to get arrested getting here, too. Did you see all those cop cars downtown?"

I think about it for a second, then remember the newscast. "It's probably all that trial stuff going on."

"Oh, right." She turns to Blake as he sits down next to me and props his feet on the bucket of balls. "Hey, Blake."

"Hey, Francesca. Thanks for coming."

"Looks like I'll be witnessing your drinking skills instead. Are you all heading to Ferg's now?"

"I think we're going to see if this passes first." I watch the puddles building on the field.

Carson dashes back into the dugout from his conference with the umpires and drips all over the equipment as he explains the situation. "We're on delay for now. They're going to see how wet the field gets."

I play along with his optimism. Most of our team has already gone to their cars to wait, but I'm not in any hurry to leave the company of my friends. I can tell that this storm isn't likely to be over fast. Anyone with a few years of Florida weather experience gets to know the difference between a quick passing shower and a prolonged storm, and this one appears to be settling in for the evening. I'm bummed to not be playing for another week, but even rainout beers are better than being at work.

"I guess those guys don't think it's going to let up," Robbie says, noting the opposing dugout clearing out.

Carson picks up his clipboard. "If it stops and they don't have enough players to re-take the field, we win by forfeit."

"I came here to play. I hate winning by forfeit," Robbie grumbles.

"What's new with you, Blake?" Francesca steers the conversation away from our glum prospects.

"Did Ben not tell you the news yet?"

"No, he's obviously slacking in the gossip department. What's your news?"

Blake looks at me. "Should I show it to her?"

"You have it with you?"

"Yeah, it's in my Jeep."

"What is it?" Francesca's curiosity is piqued.

"Be right back." Blake gets up, walks past Carson, who is in deep concentration over the stats sheet, and dashes into the rain toward the parking lot.

"What's he got?" Francesca brushes a strand of dark hair out of her eyes.

"It's pretty impressive." I grab my flip-flops out of the overhead cubbies and start changing out of my cleats.

A minute later, Blake dashes back into the dugout holding a plastic bag. He sits next to Francesca and unwraps the package, revealing a jewelry box.

"Oh for Mallory?" Francesca exclaims. Blake pries open the lid and displays the diamond ring inside. "Ooh, you did good Blake!" Francesca takes the box and looks adoringly at the ring.

"Well it's time," he replies.

"How long have you two been dating now? Four years?" Carson's interest in the statistics sheet is waning.

"Yeah, I wanted to wait till she finished grad school, but now that she's almost done, we're taking the leap."

"That's awesome, man." Robbie pats Blake on the shoulder.

We pass the ring box around, admiring it as the rain beats down on the dugout. Under the bright lights of the baseball diamond, the ring sparkles even more than the last time I saw it. *Mallory's going to love it. I need to find a ring like that. I need to find a girl like that.*

I close the ring box and pass it on to Robbie. As I do, an exceptionally bright lightning bolt sears across the sky and hits what can only be a few blocks away. The thunderclap is deafening and immediate. The bench is a symphony of expletives and Francesca clenches my arm and pulls herself against me.

"Holy shit that was close!" Robbie says.

A high-pitched whine like a jet engine begins to emanate from the direction of the strike. It grows louder and is followed by an explosion of bright blue light that domes up through the rain and illuminates the cloudy sky.

"What the hell—" is all that escapes my mouth, before a deafening bang from a transformer blowing behind us drowns me out. I'm still too startled from the shock to move when the severed end of a power line whips into the end of the dugout and lands on the far end of our bench. The last thing I sense before blacking out is the sight of my friends glowing with a pale blue light, and the sound of Francesca screaming.

I open my eyes to bleary but bright sunlight. I'm lying on my back staring at a clear blue sky. The bright light worsens the ache in my head, so I close my eyes again. I can feel the heat of the sun on my face and the dry itchy feeling of grass on my arms and the backs of my ears. There's definitely something crawling on my arm, but I'm too unmotivated to care. I monitor the slow progression of little insect feet, trying to gauge the threat. *Lady bug maybe? Spider?* I consider the most likely candidates. *Shit, if it's a fire ant, there's probably a zillion more around.* I open my eyes and angle my head slowly upward, trying to locate the intruder in the crook of my elbow. My eyes adjust to the light and I make out the ant. Not a fire ant. I lay my head back and stare at the midday sky. *Why is it daytime?*

Continue this adventure! Get *In Times Like These* free at your favorite retailer. Download Here.

ALSO BY NATHAN VAN COOPS

Ready for another adventure? Check out these books by Nathan Van Coops. Read free with Kindle Unlimited.

In Times Like These

The Chronothon

The Day After Never

Faster Than Falling

ACKNOWLEDGMENTS

Thanks for reading this novella! If you enjoyed this adventure, please consider leaving a review to tell others about your experience. This author will read it and appreciate it!

A big thank you to all the beta readers who read this story and gave me feedback. Especially those in the Facebook reader group, Beta Team Bravo. A special thank you to Emily Young, Marilyn Bourdeau, Kay Clark, Bethany Cousins, Billy Thomas, Sean Peter, Mark Hale, Ray Clements, and Dennis P. Sable for giving feedback on this novella. If you'd like to be a part of future reads and have a chance to read new books in this series first, be sure to sign up at www.nathanvancoops.com

ABOUT THE AUTHOR

Nathan Van Coops is an author, aircraft mechanic, and flight instructor in St. Petersburg, Florida. He does his best writing while eating tacos. Find out more about his real-life and fictional adventures by saying hello!

Find me here!

www.nathanvancoops.com
nathan@nathanvancoops.com